'BIYI BA

DEATH CATCHES THE HUNTER
and

ME AND THE BOYS

AMBER LANE PRESS

All rights whatsoever in these plays are strictly reserved and application for performance, etc. must be made before rehearsals begin to:
The Agency (London) Ltd
24 Pottery Lane
Holland Park
London W11 4LZ
No performance may be given unless a licence has been obtained.

First published in 1995 by
Amber Lane Press Ltd
Cheorl House
Church Street
Charlbury
Oxford OX7 3PR
Telephone: 01608 810024

Printed in Great Britain by
Bocardo Press, Didcot, Oxon

ISBN 1 872868 15 0

DEATH CATCHES THE HUNTER

Death catches the hunter with pain.
The trickster-God catches the herbalist in a sack.

Traditional

To 'Dotun

CHARACTERS

in order of appearance

SARATU – a woman who speaks in tongues
EMEFA – a prophet
PETERU – Saratu's husband and Emefa's pianist

Death Catches the Hunter was first presented by Wild Iris at the B.A.C., Battersea, London on 12 October 1995. It was directed by Polly Irvin with the following cast:

EMEFA . . . . . Chad Shepherd

PETERU . . . . . Akim Mogaji

SARATU . . . . . Adjoa Andoh

Designer: Anouk Emanuel

Lighting Designer: Paul Taylor

PROLOGUE

Lights come up on SARATU.

SARATU

[*almost as if to herself*] I'd be lying of course if I said I wasn't worried. I'd be lying. But, trying to explain Prophet Emefa's actions on that fateful day would be futile, of little help. It is, as our people say, the dog whose time has come, it will not heed the hunter's whistle. You know that story, I'm sure, about the two newly arrived colonial officers who go walking in the forest one day and come face to face with a lion. They almost run smack into the lion. And one of them says to the other: "Don't worry, old boy, I read this book once, tells you what to do if you run into a lion." "What?" says the other. "You mustn't show any fear, that's what you mustn't do. Simply turn round and walk away, that's what it says in the book." "Well," says the other, "I've also read that book. What worries me is—has this lion read it?"

I still remember that day as clearly as if it was only yesterday.

[*Pause.*]

It was breezy. The sun was blazing.

ACT ONE

Morning. The stage is dark. Whilst this darkness lasts we hear in the distance a strange but profoundly engaging piece of piano music. It is an old jazz number: James P. Johnson's 'Thou swell'.

Lights gradually come on during the first few minutes of Prophet EMEFA's speech which he begins, while intermittently humming some of the notes of the opening music. He continues his speech as he is getting changed to go out on an obviously important mission.

EMEFA is in a room in his vicarage. We should be able to see through an open window parts of the church's exterior. It is an edifice of exquisite but sombre elegance. A sign outside reads 'TRANSCENDENTAL CHURCH OF GOD, WORLD HEADQUARTERS, KAFANCHAN'. The set should be spartan rather than elaborate; symbolic rather than naturalistic.

Prophet EMEFA has a deep, thundering voice. His blistering eyes bespeak a man of steadfast and passionate beliefs. His detractors, if he has any, might even say he has the eyes of a fanatic.

EMEFA

My mother—my mother used to say to me, no matter how hard you try, you will not find God on a palm tree. Of course she meant this only in a manner of speaking. She had nothing against the palm, considering its wine to be the spittle of God: it cleansed her mind and rid my infant body of the chicken pox.

You see, I was an only child of a single mother, so you'll pardon me, I hope, if I do sometimes go on about her. Of my father, I do not know a thing. Depending on her mood—or mine—mother would often tell me that he was a bad man, or a good man. A kind man, or degenerate scum. She would say that he was alive, or that he had died before I was born. I believed her. Later in life, much later, when my calling had been revealed to me—and sanctified, my vocation divined, my gift such as it were, endorsed—it was more than a gift. It was a mission. At that point in my life, when—to my utmost horror and embarrassment—my name was being mentioned in the same breath as . . . [*makes the sign of the cross*] . . . it became fashionable among the flock to look for other parallels in both our lives. And thus the story went around that I was born in circumstances not entirely unlike Our Lord's. A virgin birth. I immediately took steps to banish this frippery from all minds. But then the thought occurred to me that, seeing that God works in mysterious ways, it could not be entirely ruled out that this legend of my virgin birth had exalted origins, had in fact been insinuated by Himself [*gestures upwards*] in the minds of my followers. For reasons best known to Him. So I refrained from intervening. I must admit that sometimes—in moments of weakness—I have actually stumbled upon myself wondering if it might not actually be true? In fun, of course, only in fun. I do not blaspheme.

Mother instilled in me the finest strictures of spiritual rigour. She believed—as I do today—that at the root of most of the world's problems was a poverty of spiritual rigour. Spiritual rigour. The word faith did not appeal to her. She preferred to say spiritual rigour. Other parents would send their children off to school with a penny in their pockets. I was lucky if I got a slap: "The Lord Jesus Christ went forty days and forty nights without so much as a drop of water, and you fret about missing *one* meal!

Where is your spiritual rigour, young man?" Not that I minded, please note, not that I minded.

She taught me respect. Complete and utter respect. When once I made a rude remark about a rather unpleasant neighbour of ours—to her, in his absence, in the privacy of our home—she caught hold of my ear and dragged me down the street to the man's door. "I shall not have a disrespectful child under my roof," she announced as she rapped on the door with her knuckles. For one terrible moment I thought she'd dragged me here to give me away. When the man finally came to the door and opened it, it was with the utmost consternation that he stared at the two of us, mother and child, looking—I suppose—like street urchins on an evening romp. "Mr Ajudikudi," mother said, "Emefa has come to apologise." And I did indeed apologise. I had scarcely finished doing this when Mother swung me round and propelled me back in the direction of home. One of my abiding memories is that of Mr Ajudikudi that night, standing in the doorway, his balding head shining dangerously in the sun, looking absolutely bewildered. He never did summon the courage to ask me or my mother why on earth I'd come to apologise that day. For my part, I'd learnt the real meaning of respect.

[*He hums.*]

You'd have gathered by now that I'm—shall we say—a man of the cloth. You would be right if you put it in those terms. I mean to say, not far from the truth. But to say that I am a man of God is to speak in rather generic terms. To scratch the surface, as the saying goes. Or as my mother would say, to see only the froth on top of the palm wine.

[*emphatically*] I did not choose to be a prophet. I did not wake up one morning and decide to be a prophet. [*chuckles*] I know, I know . . .[*that it's amusing*]. A contradiction in terms. One has no choice in these matters. I can say right now, with all confidence and without fear of contradiction, that in certain matters even God does not practise democracy. Instance: I had no wish to be a prophet.

> [*A roar from a distance. Possibly from farther even than the piano music. It is the roar of an animal. The sound catches* EMEFA *slightly off-guard. He falters momentarily then smiles almost sheepishly.*]

We—um—our local zoo. That roar, that was the lion.

SARATU

They say that on the day Ogun came down from his hill, he was clothed in fire and wore a garment of blood; he borrowed palm fronds from palm trees and entered the town and was immediately proclaimed king. So with Prophet Emefa on the day he came back to Kafanchan. The thing about the prophet is—I suppose—his . . . humility . . . that was what convinced me of his true divinity. Like Ogun, like Jesus Christ . . .

It might also have something to do with his humble beginnings, of course.

Take his father, for instance. He was a right monster, they said. He worked with the railways, same as everybody else in town. On the lines, same as my father, and Peteru's father too. But that man, the prophet's father, they say he . . .

> [*She grasps for the word she wants but gives up.*]

They say that the only accident that ever happened to him was the accident of being sober. They say he used to beat the prophet's mother to nonsense. He would come home drunk every night. Sometimes he wouldn't even bother coming home at all, but whenever he did it was pure hell for the woman. She'd lost most of her teeth before she was thirty. He'd punched them out of her mouth. Yet she didn't leave him. She didn't leave him. In those days it was simply inconceivable that a woman should leave her marital home on the flimsy grounds that her husband saw fit to give her a thumping now and again. How else would he show that he cared for her?

He finally dropped dead, of course. Something to do with his liver being eaten out by . . . well, one swig too many.

I've never heard the prophet talk about him. No, I tell a lie. I've heard him talk about him to journalists, many times. And it's always the same story: "I was the only child of a single mother". The first time I heard him say that I thought, what is he . . . [*talking about*]? Then I said to myself, so be it. If that's what he says, that's what it is. Maybe it's because of the way the man treated his mother. They say the prophet really hated him. I mean, even his name proves it: Emefa. That's it: Emefa. People sometimes think it's his surname. It isn't. It's his first name. He doesn't have a surname. And I ask myself, could he have hated his father to that extent? I don't think so. If there's anybody in this world who doesn't have the capacity to hate another person it's Prophet Emefa.

Yet any time the journalists ask him, he says "I was the only child of a single mother."

EMEFA

I had no wish to be . . . [*a prophet*]. The calling came to me one afternoon while I was on the tenth floor of my Lagos Island suite of offices. I had recently successfully concluded a most rewarding case involving one of the wealthiest people this side of our hemisphere. I had behind me an impeccable—others would say brilliant—record as a defence lawyer, commanded the highest rates in the profession and had just been invested with a chieftaincy by the people of my mother's home town. "In recognition of your shining accomplishments in your field of endeavour" read the citation, if I rightly remember. I felt honoured.

Mother giggled like a baby throughout the ceremony. I'd never seen her look so at peace with the world. It was as if this was the moment she'd been waiting for all her life. Not even when I was called to the bar had she looked so content. It was in a way her finest hour.

She passed away shortly afterwards. In her sleep. I never knew how old she was. She hadn't the faintest idea either. She used to say that she was born in the Year of the Salt Shortage. When she died, she was the happiest toothless old woman that had ever lived.

And so I was in my Lagos office that bitterly hot afternoon, counting my blessings, seeing that I was in splendidly air-conditioned surroundings so that it wasn't so bitterly hot . . . And looking down to the street at some of the flotsam and jetsam of the city, who were, at that moment, undoubtedly feeling bitterly hot, I felt blessed. I mean to say, blessed and humbled with gratitude.

It was at that moment—as I stared down the Marina, ten storeys in the direction of heaven . . . that I—let me tell you exactly how it happened . . . I looked emptily down the busy street beside the Marina. You know the one of which I speak: just in front of the General Post Office, straddled between the funeral parlour and the cathedral. One for the body, one for the soul, we used to say of those two buildings. The funeral parlour and the cathedral. In jest, of course. Only in jest. As I looked down, I saw—it remains in my mind's eye as vivid as if it happened only yesterday—a man. It could have been a woman, but it wasn't . . . It could even have been a child, but it wasn't . . . It was—a man. I saw a man. There were five, possibly ten thousand people on that street that afternoon. Some smiling, some clearly unhappy with the cost—not to mention the standard—of living. Some in love—mostly with themselves . . . From this multitude, a man, whom I'd never seen before—and haven't seen since—stood out. My eyes, of their own will, of their own seeking, found him out.

He was an old man, thin—wizened, I should say—with . . . well, what else but . . . poverty. He must have been all of seventy if he was a day. And then again, he could have been a mere forty. He must have once been a tall man. No longer. He looked now like . . . [*curves his body forward in demonstration*] . . . an Iroko branch you bend to make a hunter's bow. His face was botched up, swollen with red patches like one afflicted with cirrhosis of the liver, and yet shrivelled like smoked fish. He walked—or, more appropriately, dragged one foot after the other in a pathetic imitation of the act of walking.

Ten storeys high I was and yet I saw him as clearly as if he had been right there within reach of my arm. I could see every little fold in his skin, every spot, every mosquito bite, every knife scar. He had a staff, of course. He looked as if he would cave in—miss a step and fall flat on his face if he didn't have the staff. I sat forward and looked more closely at him. I looked at his face, the relics of it, and observed that he'd lost his teeth—all of them. He chewed his kola nut still, though, grinding it into a fine paste with the rough side of a milk tin into which holes had been punched. I looked at his eyes—he had none. It dawned upon me that the man was blind.

I had come across blind mendicants in the past, note, please. I assuaged my conscience by bringing out my wallet every time I chanced by a beggar, which wasn't that often come to think of it. [*self-mockingly*] The clubs to which I belonged had stringent membership requirements, you see. And the circles within which I moved . . . I mean to say, it wasn't as if I deliberately avoided beggars. Far from it. Indeed, I was committed to a few deserving charitable causes . . .

An alien force, a force stronger than myself, appeared to yank me out of my seat. One moment I was . . . [*takes on executive sitting posture*] . . . the next . . . [*literally flies out of his invisible chair*] And suddenly I'd brushed past my secretary and was dashing furiously down the stairs. The lift was there. In fact there were two. It did not even cross my mind that I might use them. Perhaps I was possessed? I felt that I was being led by the arm. By whom or what, I could not say. I raced down the stairs, leaping, taking the steps two at a go. Effortlessly, absolutely effortlessly. And that, at a time when the nearest I'd come to being religious was in my unfaltering faithfulness to a regimen of sixty a day. In the days before the packets began bearing those health warnings, too.

I was not even panting when I reached the ground floor. Three-piece and all and dashing like a spirit through the crowded lounge. They all thought I'd gone unhinged.

The sun hit me full blast in the face as I came out of the building and into the street. But I did not so much as falter. The blind beggar was only a few metres away. I narrowly missed being run over by a bus as I sprinted across the road to get to the old man. And then . . . I reached him. I was there, standing in front of him and taking hold of his hand.

Obviously the man had seen a lot in his time. He'd seen enough of humanity to lose any shadow of trust he might have had in him. He screamed when I took hold of his hand. He screamed in a voice that cut like a knife through the thronged street. He thought he was being attacked.

I laid my hand firmly upon his forehead and commanded his eyes to open, his vision to return. I said this casually, quietly in fact, in the way one says "Excuse me, have you got the right time?" to a stranger in the street.

Slowly, very slowly, they came open. His eyes, sightless since the day he was born, came alive. He took one step backward, and then one step forward. He could not—but who would in their right senses—believe his eyes. He looked at me. Up, and then down. Several times. Then he flung away his staff and commenced a frenzied dance of joy.

I, for my part, was in shock. I realised what had happened but refused to believe it. It was not in my interest to believe it. It was another miracle that I managed to leave the scene that day without being mobbed. The crowd was as dazed as I.

SARATU

At the time his mother left Kafanchan, shortly after his father's funeral, he had not shown any signs of his future

vocation. None at all. At least no-one seems to remember.
And in this town people have a way of never forgetting
things. It's so small, see. You could walk its length and
breadth in less time than it takes to get a taxi in Lagos.
It's just the railways we have here. That's where most of
the men work. The railways, the government ministries,
the schools—and the churches.

I don't know why the prophet decided to come back here
and set up his. I tell a lie. I mean, I've guessed many
times: it must be that sad business about his mother—
when she died. It really knocked him for six, they say—
those who knew him in Lagos.

That's something else he never talks about. I'll always
say this of Prophet Emefa: he's a holy man, a divine man,
cures the afflicted, has raised the dead. But leave him
alone to blow his nose and you've got the makings of a
major disaster. He brings strength to those beaten by
life, joy to the unhappy, hope to the disillusioned, laughter to cheeks that have only known tears. You'd think a
person like that would be glowing with happiness, not
so? Not so?

His mother, when she left here, took him to Lagos.
Slaved for him, that's what she did—to give him a decent
education. She did all sorts of things, that woman:
worked at the docks, on construction sites, cleaned
streets . . . Anything to bring in the odd penny, anything
to pay the rent, pay her son's school fees. She was—
determined . . . There've been slanders, of course, lies,
wicked lies . . . that she became a . . . [*prostitute*] in order
to survive . . . Lies, pure lies. That's something else about
this town. [*loud whisper*] They lie a lot.

She never lived to reap the fruits of her labour. Barely a
week before he graduated from Law School—he was

training to be a lawyer—she suddenly fell ill. Just past middle age at this time, they say. Looked a hundred. All that suffering, you see. Barely a week from his graduation from Law School, she fell ill and died.

EMEFA

That night, in the middle of the night, as I rolled restlessly on my bed, I fell into a vision.

SARATU

And that was it for him: he simply *walked*. One more week. One single week more and he would have walked out of that school a fully fledged lawyer. But no, he took his mother back to her village and buried her there . . . and walked. He loved that woman, he really did.

But God works in mysterious ways. The prophet—not yet prophet at this time, but soon to be, soon to be—went on a long trek of bereavement. He went without food or water for weeks at a stretch, sleeping rough, lying where the night found him, moving in whatever direction the wind blew him. He was robbed by bandits and brutalised by the law, welcomed in many places and turned away in sundry villages. This was when he began to commune with himself, to speak from within the deepest recesses of his being . . .

The world thought at this time that he had gone mad. His father's people pointed fingers at his mother's people. His mother's people turned back to them and said, why have you done this to him? He did fool them all. For he was not mad: when you see a person walking naked on the street, speaking within to themselves, don't call them mad. You could be in the presence of a messenger of God . . .

EMEFA

A shaft of light came bursting through the ceiling. I shielded my eyes with a pillow, to keep from being blinded. A voice spoke to me from this fastness of light. I did not hear it with my ears, rather I felt it in my head. The words seeped into me as water into the earth. The voice said to me: "Depart from Lagos. Go to a place called Kafanchan." "Lord," I said, "where is this place called Kafanchan and what shall I find there?" I knew He was given to a sharp sense of wit but the brevity of the answer to my query had me . . . [*mouth agape*] "Get a map." I did as I was told.

"Now go there and build a church to glorify my name. You shall be gifted with the gift of miracles. You shall cure the afflicted and give life to the ill."

I was told to look out for a sign. Not the sign of Jonah, but the sign of the froth. Those were the words. The sign of the froth.

I gave away my money, all my property, resigned from the practice—there was talk of getting me to see a psychiatrist. [*laughs*] I packed a bag one night, a small bag containing one shirt, one pair of trousers, chewing stick, a copy of the Holy Book. And stepped into the dawn.

SARATU

His journey took him to many places, many regions within our earth. He met Gods and infidels, angels and djinns of mischief.

The first God he met was Eshu, the God of fate, the one who turns right into wrong and wrong into right, the one who throws a stone today and kills a bird yesterday.

Eshu blessed him. And as a parting gift, gave him powers.

The second God he met was Shango, the God of thunder. He walks alone, but enters the town like a swarm of locusts. His feet are like the crab's, walking in many directions at the same time. Shango is the one who went to Ibadan—and arrived in Ilorin. He was on a farm when the bereaved man met him, kneeling down, like a collector of vegetables. But Shango does not collect vegetables. He's only looking for the head of the farmer. Shango blessed him. And as a parting gift, gave him powers.

The third God he met was Soponna, God of the pox. Soponna blessed him. And gave him powers.

He met Oya, Goddess of the river, of strong winds, lightning and fire. The one who heals the barren woman with honey and cures with water. Oya is the one who guards the path into the world and the road out of it. He steeped his feet in the warmth of Oya and felt her blessings wash away his aches. She gave him powers.

He met Ogun as well; the one who kills the child with the iron with which it plays. The one who kills the thief and the owner of the stolen goods. Ogun has water but he bathes in blood. Ogun blessed him. And gave him powers.

Then he went further and came face to face with Obatala, the creator. Obatala blessed him. And as a parting gift, gave him powers.

And as he went on his wanderings, speaking to deep silences, hosted by Gods and courted by spirits, it rained heavily one night and he sheltered in a church. And that night also he met with another God . . .

EMEFA

There was a definite spring in my steps as I walked that morning. I must confess that my eagerness to heed this call was influenced in no little way by the promise of infinite power it held. In the spiritual sense, I mean to say.

> [*He pauses to listen to the pianist who has again begun to play 'Thou Swell'. He ums and ahs in approval and nods in the direction from which the music is coming.*]

Peteru our pianist. He keeps on playing that because he knows it to be one of my all-time favourite pieces of music. I suppose it's his way of saying he's worried. As to what he is worried about, I haven't a clue. [*hums*] I taught him that, you know, to play the piano. He was—him and his wife, Saratu—among my first converts when I came to Kafanchan. A good man, that Peteru. An unrepentant sinner, sure to perish in hell, but essentially a good man. As to his wife Saratu, she . . . On my first day in the town she offered me the answer to a mystery. It was my first crusade in town. I'd gone around posting bills on walls, on trees in the streets, asking them all to bring their ill and afflicted ones. I promised miraculous healings through . . . I used the words, spiritual rigour.

SARATU

On the day Emefa came back to Kafanchan he was dressed in a coat of rags and his hair was caked with dirt and there were lice on the shirt that he wore. The town would have turned its back on him but for the incident with the blind old man he met on the road that veers down the hill near the cemetery. He placed a finger on the old man's eyes, they say, and—there were witnesses, scores of witnesses—the man suddenly found himself with sight. He'd been born blind, this man. Had never seen the light of day before. And suddenly he could see. That old man was my father-in-law, Peteru's father. We'd been married only two years at the time, Peteru and I. Quite happily, with no more than our fair share of ups and downs, but really, quite happily. I was a teacher at the time at a local High School. Peteru was a mechanic, owned his own workshop, even employed others to work for him. In those days being a teacher had the prestige value of being an army officer today. Being a mechanic meant money.

We were quite happy, really, saving towards a house, planning on having our first baby . . . This second, with a great deal of anxiety . . . I'd been told at the hospital that I had to be very careful. I was ill, you see.

EMEFA

The gathering took place at the football pitch of a local primary school. I still remember the spot today even though it has been overrun by the public cemetery. There was a blind man present. And a woman paralysed from the waist. Two barren women, an infertile man and one whose wife said he was impotent. And then there was— Saratu . . .

Epilepsy, her husband said.

[PETERU *steps out in front of* EMEFA.]

PETERU

She foams at the mouth, Prophet.

EMEFA

He said to me in utter despair. "She does?" I said to him.

[PETERU *leaves.*]

SARATU

Sometimes I would go for years without experiencing a single attack. Other years I would have one almost every other month. The year the prophet came was one of those years. It was the major blight of our lives. So when Peteru's father came home that evening—we were still living in the family compound at the time—with his eyes . . . and told us the incredible news, we could hardly contain our excitement. Perhaps this was the answer? It wasn't difficult tracking down the mangy-haired stranger—we weren't to know until much later that he was actually born local—we were told he was holding a crusade that evening on the football pitch of the school. People couldn't figure out what kind of crusade it was, but it isn't every day that you run into someone who makes the blind see . . .

And so there we were that evening, Peteru, myself and his whole family . . . There were twenty, maybe twenty-five people there that night. Most of them had come more out of curiosity than anything else. There should've been more but it was one of those periods in Kafanchan when almost everyone had recently become an ex-churchgoer: Father O'Donnel's church from which members had defected *en masse* because the Latin mass went above their heads, now held its services in English, Hausa, Igbo and Yoruba. This proved to be a mistake; now that they could understand what was being said, even more people left. On the other hand, Prophet Jeremiah—and two other 'prophets' who had attracted members by getting popular musicians to make cameo appearances and by funkifying church hymns—were now in jail for fraud and embezzlement.

So it wasn't a particularly good time for churches when Prophet Emefa came to town . . . About twenty-five people came to his crusade that night. A few, like myself, with physical ailments. I remember some of the others. There was Baba Ingila, struck from childhood with the river blindness. What he lacked in sight, he made up for in speech. He had been known to hold shebeen audiences enthralled with his long, endless stories. He would begin them late in the evening and inch towards the middle at dawn the following day when every one of his listeners had either nodded off or been dragged home by their wives. He had been forced to the crusade that night by friends. His face was set in a bemused mask.

There were also two barren women, a paralysed woman, a man whose seeds never seemed strong enough and another who'd been dragged there by his wife on the grounds that he was totally useless in bed.

Everyone there that night was healed except for the man who was useless in bed. He was later caught on top of another man.

As for me that night, I was a wreck of nerves . . . I usually was on occasions such . . . [*as that*]. And the tension would sometimes induce an attack. That was precisely what happened. It happened suddenly. So suddenly in fact that I was only aware that it'd happened after it was over. My head ached, as it usually did after I'd had an attack. I felt numb in the mouth, I ran my tongue over my teeth—or rather, my teeth over my tongue—to make sure that I hadn't bitten off a bit of it during the attack. I'd been laid out on a blanket in the middle of the gathering. In the mist before my eyes I could see my husband hovering anxiously behind Prophet Emefa who

stood before me with a look approaching wonder on his
face . . .

SARATU — no

EMEFA

I was instructed to look out for the sign of the froth.

SARATU

He said mysteriously—

EMEFA

This—

SARATU

He pointed at me.

EMEFA

Is the sign of the froth.

SARATU

He turned to Peteru and said to him—

[PETERU *appears*.]

EMEFA

[*to* PETERU] Your wife is blessed, sir, not afflicted.

SARATU

The crowd looked on in utter puzzlement. I hadn't a clue
either.

EMEFA

Observe the spittle that came forth from her mouth,
consider the frenzy which engulfed her body, note the
twitching of her face, how her teeth chattered and her
tongue tried to turn on its back . . .

[*Pause.*]

Those endowed with this—condition—should by right and purpose be the voices of God amongst us. Their spittle is like the froth on palm wine. It is a subtle promise of great things beneath. Their true ailment is that their gift is not complete. They have all the qualities of a seer of visions—except talking in tongues.

SARATU

Except for the moon there were no lights that night on the football pitch where we were gathered. But even in the near darkness the prophet's face was clearly etched out as he bent down to place a hand on my forehead. His eyes blazed as they do even today. Like a piercing light into hidden secrets.

[*Pause.*]

That night I spoke in tongues and communed with presences. I spoke for Gods and kindly spirits. I was rendered—complete.

[*Fade to black.*]

END OF ACT ONE

ACT TWO

Evening. Darkness on stage. As in Act One we hear strains from 'Thou Swell'.

We are in another room in the vicarage. As the lights come on we see a gigantic piano on stage. It should require quite a diligent eye to realise that there is a man seated at this formidable object.

PETERU *is a short, impish fellow with a deceptively slight figure, almost lethargic even. Not to be fooled: he possesses the energy of a town-crier and the self-assured tenacity of a muezzin at the dawn call to prayer. He emits malice in carefully measured doses. But beneath this he is a regular fellow, possibly likeable.*

PETERU

Yes, sir. . . That was his all-time favourite tune of all . . .

> [*It should gradually become apparent that he is speaking not to the audience but to a group of people in front of him on stage. He dishes out a brief further sampling.*]

'Thou Swell' it is called . . . Yes, 'Thou Swell'. T-h-o-u S-w-e-l-l . . . Excuse me, sir . . . [*leans over to take a peep at a notebook*] . . . Mustn't get the spelling wrong or the prophet will be . . . He's very particular, you see, especially with little things like this. Very particular . . . And I tell you, sometimes it has occurred to me that it might actually be easier for a camel to go through the eye of a needle than for it to catch Prophet Emefa's eye of approval . . . No, no, excuse me please, that was meant to

be off the record actually, thank you . . . I mean, I vividly
remember his asking me once in that very deep and
authoritative voice of his: "Brother Peteru," he said to
me, "why, after all these years of making your acquain-
tance, have I not been able to convince myself that your
intellect isn't only as tall as your stature?" And over
what? Ask me over what? Because I was playing him his
beloved 'Thou Swell' and missed a note. One note. And
he calls me an idiot! But then even Our Lord Jesus Christ
was known to have a temper—beating up all those people
in the temple and all that business. I mean, gambling or
no gambling, they were only after their daily bread . . .
With all due respect, that one na consecrated thuggery.
Now, understand me, please, ladies . . . gents . . . I'm not
complaining at all. Put that in italics: *Brother Peteru says
I am not complaining* . . . I mean, fifteen years I was with
him, fifteen years I worked for him: pianist, personal
assistant, secretary, right-hand man . . . Cured my wife
of—well, you know that story. Gave sight to my father.
And also taught me everything I know today . . . everything. I mean, what was I before Prophet Emefa came
along? Common mechanic. I was making good money all
right, no doubt about that, had a nice wife—stubborn but
nice . . . But that's not all life is about, is it? Prophet
Emefa came along and taught me how to be like high
society. First he tried to teach me his big, big grammar
but there he fell flat on his face. Me and book have never
seen eye to eye. That is why my father withdrew me from
school after Standard Five and put me under apprentice-
ship. De boy is good motor mechanics. De Boy is Good.
That was when I discovered my true calling in this world.
[*wistfully*] I was a wizard with vehicles. Even the boss,
Mechanical Monsoon—his real name was Monsur but he
thought Monsoon sounded better so he changed his name

—even he sometimes 'bowed' to me. He would call me and hand over the keys . . . And one hour later, wetin you go see? Passenger bus working regular as clockwork. And that was the same me who thought Pythagoras theorem na brand name for whisky . . .

Now, where was I? Oh, yes, Prophet Emefa was wonderful man o . . . You say what? I no hear you . . . You need photographs to go with your exclusives? [*chuckles*] How many of you de do exclusive self? Okay, you who is wanting photographs make una give me just a minute . . .

> [*He changes into a cassock and puts a crucifix around his neck. He brings out a couple of spectacle cases and tries on a pair of glasses.*]

Prophet say de reason he couldn't abracadabra away my own eye problem be say I be man of spiritual rigor mortis. That means man of no faith. Maybe he's right. But I suspect that the real reason is because . . . [*tries on another pair of glasses*] Even God himself will confuse when he look my eye. You see this my left eye? Them say is short-sighted. [*tries on the first pair again*] You see this one? [*gestures at his right eye*] Them say na long-sighted. Sometimes the problems swap places. Prophet Emefa called my condition a miracle in itself. [*finally settles on the second pair*] Okay now, ladies and gentlemen, snap away.

> [*A blackout, then a series of 'camera flashes' each revealing* PETERU *in varying postures. This is best realised perhaps by running a succession of slide-shots of* PETERU *in the different poses: sorrowful; pathetic; in prayer; clutching at a bible; behind the piano; in front of the piano; caught in mid-speech, etc.*]

[*Lights come on.*]

That should do for now, gentlemen and ladies. I'm afraid that's all the time I can spare with you.

[*He extends his hand for handshakes and exchanges pleasantries as each of the journalists takes their leave. When he has seen the last one out he goes back to the door and calls out to someone.*]

Okay now, the coast is clearer, you can bring your cameras in here . . . And I'm only doing this for you, my man . . . Only for you. I wouldn't accept that kind of pittance from anyone else. Believe me, sir, I've made double this amount in hours during the prophet's most prolific days of miracle cures. The queues used to stretch right from the gates out there straight through past the cinema house on the end of town. All seeking one cure or the other: from chronic piles to involuntary flatulence, we had all sorts in front of those gates, I tell you. From all over the country too. In fact sef, from all over the world. And I'd go about with a collection bowl, getting the miserable bastards to make a small 'contribution'. It was easier squeezing water out of stone. Anyway, just carry your equipments enter one time make I lock the door . . . Are you sure you've really got my wife adequately cornered by your other colleagues . . . because if she walks in here right this moment she'll be sweeping even your footprints out through that door . . . Yes, Mr Cameraman, you can put up your lights there . . .

[*A sharp television studio light comes up each time he points.*]

And there and there . . . and maybe here . . .

[*He sits on a stool at the piano. As he begins the following speech the concentration of lights on him endows him with almost sepulchral greyness. He has become sorrow personified. He speaks now, ostensibly to the 'cameras' but actually to the audience.*]

I'm still in shock. My hands tremble and my voice shakes. I hope you'll forgive me if sometimes I become incoherent. But that would be because I'm in deep, deep shock. I suppose the most painful thing is that only a few hours ago he was here with us. As always, smiling. As always kind, benevolent, cheerful and big-hearted, a fine man, a complete gentleman. Only this morning we were talking about the greatest love of his life, aside from God, that is: music.

When my wife and I first had the privilege of meeting him a little over fifteen years ago . . . Let me tell you about that before I go any further . . . I met Prophet Emefa for the first time one moonlit night here in Kafanchan on the football pitch of the then St Peter's Primary School. Now that I think of it, it's rather ironic really because we shall be taking leave of him—or rather his remains—on that same football pitch in a few days from now. You see, the school is no longer there and the football pitch is now a cemetery . . .

When he first asked us—my dear wife and I—to join him in founding his church that night, he'd just cured my father of blindness, my wife of epilepsy . . . I—I was lost for words. For one thing, I didn't feel that I was exactly worthy of such an—honour. I wasn't that much of a churchgoer myself—not because I didn't believe in going to church, but because Sundays were my only day off from work.

Quite honestly, left to me, I'd never have agreed—to joining in founding the church I mean. But who was I to argue with a divine emanation such as Prophet Emefa?

I was no match for his powers of persuasion . . . And when Saratu threatened to leave me if . . . Looking back now, I thank God that I'd gone with her. It seems like yesterday now when we sat down—the three of us—to form this church that day fifteen years ago . . . not even the prophet himself had an inkling that it was going to grow this big—with all these branches all over the country . . .

His background, as we all know, was humble. He was the only son of a single mother—a godly and astute woman who brought up her son from the meagre income she made as a palm wine seller.

Prophet Emefa died as he lived: brave, holy, kind, selfless, the best friend anybody could wish for, but . . . the Lord giveth and the Lord taketh away . . . We shall miss you, prophet. May your sacred soul rest in perfect peace.

[*The 'studio' lights go out.* PETERU *visibly relaxes.*]

Satisfied? Enough? Good.

[*He lights a cigarette, looking furtively around him as he does this. He sees the television crew to the door.*]

I trust that you have filmed him already. Pity, not much of him left to film. Pity . . . Oh, no mention, my privilege really . . . When you say you'd be showing that on our screens?. . . Tonight? I'll be sure to catch it . . .

[*He goes back and takes his position on the stool at the piano.*]

Rubbish. Absolute rubbish. You should feel ashamed of yourself, Peteru. I tell you. I mean, why didn't you just tell it as it is? I mean, let's face facts. Why did he do it in the first place? He had everything going for him: the Gods, or Jesus Christ, or whoever gave him those powers he had—were still with him . . . I mean, listen . . . I admit

I was never really able to get myself to believe in all that mumblo-jumblo. Is just that I'm not cut out for that kind of thing. It's not as if I didn't try. God knows I tried. I tried to believe. But . . . What I'm saying is . . . in spite of that, I respect the man. I've come across preachers in my time, believe me. I've known common criminals laying claim to all sorts of powers. Fraudsters. Take Prophet Jeremiah, for instance. Knocked up ten of his members, including two who were married, before he finally got sent where he belonged: Kirikiri Maximum Security . . .

I must admit I was a bit wary myself when Prophet Emefa first invited Saratu and me to come set up the church with him. I know say him na holy man of course, after all, I'd just seen him in action. But still. There was the matter of his sudden interest in my wife.

I mean, I know say he cure am of epilepsy—and he did too, you know. I didn't really believe it that night. But she hasn't had another attack since. Not one. Only the other kind, the one they call being in the spirit. Then they start talking all kinds of holy *jagbajantis*. Saratu once tell me say 'e fit be say the language when dem de speak when dem de in the spirit na Hebrew. Anyway, me I tell Prophet Emefa say thank you very much, when he invite Saratu and myself, I tell him, thank you very many, but no . . . I tell you, I didn't like the way he kept looking at Saratu. The man was just gushing over her, kept going on about how spiritual she be, how she be voice of God . . . Now, that really got me worried. Because that was how Prophet Jeremiah seduced his members . . . That man! He get charm for mouth . . . And so I was very suspicious of Prophet Emefa at first . . . very suspicious.

> [*He lights another cigarette. His tone is very intimate.*]

For five whole years I de take eye follow that man . . .
Five years I de study am . . . I de wait for di day when he
go take hand touch my wife. Before God and man: I for
cut him prick. For five years I watched his every movement: when he de eat o, when he de sleep, when he de
preach, when he go toilet, when he de do those him
miracles . . . I just de watch am. I de watch am. As I de
watch him na so I de watch her. It wasn't easy, I tell you.
Not at all at all. And na dis stupid piano business cause
make the thing hard so. Because why? Because I was
always being tucked behind this thing while the two of
them was doing spiritual inside holy chamber for yonder
. . . [*gestures vaguely*] Performing miracles. Or rather she
saw the visions, and he did the miracles. My own was to
belt out one spiritual tune after the other. He call it
immaculate division of labour. Me I call it nonsense and
ingredients. I mean, how was I to know whether on any
of those plentiful occasions when I was playing 'Nearer
My Lord to Thee' that it wasn't to their 'Nearer My Hips
to Thine'?

Sometimes I would sneak into that so-called holy chamber; I would go tip and toe and tip and toe, very quietly,
very, very quietly, I would move under cover of the night,
and believe you me, before God and man, as I small so,
I fit to move like cat. Every single time when I do it I go
de pray for my mind say make God let me catch them.
Make he just let me catch them one time. But as I stand
one night with this prayer in my mind it suddenly occur
to me say I actually didn't know what I would have did
if I catch them. This shocked me deeply and unhappy me
that night. I stayed awake all night thinking. Then it
occurred to me say should in case that I catch them is
finish I go finish the two both of them. I go finish the two
both of them one time. Before God and man.

But did I ever catch them? For where! I go burst into that holy chamber of a place for t'ree o'clock a.m. for morning what would I see? She rolling on the floor like a worm you throw in salt and speaking all this nonsense and ingredient language which even God cannot fit to understand. And him? He go just stand there like stone, his eyes shut, perfectly still like one of those blind beggars you find at railway stations. They called this night vigil. They would have other 'elders' of the church in other rooms, all blabbing away in prayer. Their prayer, that one na another matter altogether. Even the neighbouring church, the Holy Order of Flying Angels and Miraculous Apostles owned by the Prophet Jeremiah was no match for the heavenly pandemonium that characterised our night vigils. Sometimes when I watch them shouting so vigorously and shaking like leaf I would be wondering if they think that God would hear them if they shouted loud enough.

Meanwhile, me I just de watch prophet and my wife. One day, one day . . . By this time the church had grown like no man's business. Before God and man, me I haven't seen such phenomenal growth before . . . I mean, we began with a shack, for God's sake . . . A shack. Right on this spot it was, where the piano room is. On this very spot. We began with less than twenty members . . . There was a big problem about the name Prophet chose—Transcendental . . . Nobody except Prophet and Saratu could pronounce it. Even me self, it took me years to learn to pronounce am. After that there was the argument about music: which kind music we go de play? Prophet talk say na jazz . . . I laugh on the day he said it. Jazz? . . . I say, Prophet, which one be this jazz? He carry record put for turntable . . . James P. Johnson . . . 'Thou Swell' recorded twenty-seven March Nineteen-Twenty-Hate. Dem write am for the album jacket. As the record de play and I stand de listen my mouth just open yau like dis . . . I no understand di thing at all. Even self 'e just be like noise for my ear. I say Prophet—I was very serious—I say Prophet, I respect you, I know that you have read plenty book more than myself, so I respect you very plenty, okay? But I must tell you true where true must be tell: nobody go come dis our church if you play dat kind music. Before God and man. Even Saratu agree with me . . . But that prophet man? He stubborn like goat. He went and buy piano come from Lagos then he come tell me, he say Peteru—he started calling me Peter at one point, but stopped when me too I started calling him Proph—he say Peteru, you will be our pianist. I say me, pianist . . . Prophet, I sure say you de joke . . . Pianist? He say, yes Peteru, I'll teach you . . . And like joke, like joke I did learn it . . .

Within five years—five years, I tell you—we had run all the other churches in town out of business. I mean it: they simply all went bankrupt and shut down. Every single one of them. I tell you, just under five years we had everybody in town absconding from dem former churches and joining us. Prophet call am carpet-crossing. Even one or two mosques were forced to close shop. That Prophet Emefa? He was a strong man, proper proper.

There were whole weeks when we hardly ever slept an hour between the three of us and the others Prophet later invited to help run the Church . . . It was miracles galore: miracles right, left and centre. The only thing he didn't quite do was walk on water. And that was because he didn't want to show off.

Those reporters just now, they were asking me, why did he do it . . . ? Outside, right now . . . Yes, you just step out there and you'll find the place is packed with the biggest crowd you ever saw, all crying their eyes out . . . And they are asking the same question: why . . . ? Not, why did he do it, but, why did it happen . . . ?

Yes, what was I saying . . . ? Why did he do it? If I told them out there what I think they'll never believe me, them fit even lynch me . . . I began to suspect a long time ago, that time almost ten years ago, when I finally convinced myself that the man genuinely had no interest in . . . sex . . . whatsoever . . . Before God and man, I no fit understand am at all . . . All he ever did seem to enjoy was his— healing . . . and his music . . . Nothing more, nothing else . . . I come ask myself, I say which kind person be this one? I mean, even Jesus Christ self 'e let Mary Magdalene rub him leg. I'm not saying he touched her, don't get me wrong, but when she was running her hands over his legs I wonder what was running through his mind at that moment . . .

So I was greatly puzzle. Then I realise one day that . . . he himself, he no know what to do with his powers. He'd become, at this time, the best known Man of God in this country . . . his fame had spread, as we say, like wild fire for harmattan . . . People were coming from all over the world—all over the whole wide world—to seek cures from him . . . And rarely did they go disappointed. He had—power . . . That was his whole passion in life: that power to do and undo . . . That was all that interested him, nothing else . . . Not woman, or man, or money, or anything self . . . In a way, he don begin think say him be God. He fit do anything. He lived, in a way, only for the next miracle . . . And then, the next miracle sudden became only the next miracle . . . And he got bored . . .

And that's why he did what he did today.

[*heavenwards*] May your soul rest in peace, Prophet Emefa.

[*He lights another cigarette.*]

God knows I had nothing but good thoughts for him. Only at the beginning, when I thought he was after Saratu.

[*Thoughtful pause. He brings out a cut-throat knife that had been strapped to his knee and lays it down on the piano.*]

God is my witness, if he'd made a move on her, if I'd so much as seen him near her, I for just cut him prick one time no delay. Make we see whether he go gum the thing back with miracle.

[*Instant blackout.*]

END OF ACT TWO

ACT THREE

Midday. We are back in the room in Act One. EMEFA *is getting to his feet from kneeling in front of a mini-altar.* SARATU *is standing by the window, her back to us.*

EMEFA

And how are they faring now?

SARATU

Twice as many as when I looked a few minutes ago. It's strange, the look on their faces. Calm, relaxed. Some have even come with their families. They've spread out mats, brought food. They might as well be out on a picnic.

EMEFA

That's what I call faith, sister. Spiritual rigour. They have complete trust. That's more than can be said for some people we know around here . . .

SARATU

[*heatedly*] I made clear my feelings about the matter when you made the announcement . . .

EMEFA

I made no announcement, sister. You were there. Some-one went into the spirit . . .

SARATU

I know I went into the spirit, Prophet. But I had mes-sages for several people that day. I spoke in tongues, you could have misinterpreted . . .

EMEFA

You underestimate your own gifts, sister. I know a
volcano when I see one. I know an eruption when I'm
standing in the middle of it.

SARATU

But you have said it yourself: these things can be wrongly
interpreted . . .

EMEFA

I did not misinterpret. I do not misinterpret . . .

[SARATU *looks out of the window again.*]

SARATU

It's almost time. They're looking this way now. They're
waiting for you.

[EMEFA *stands up.*]

EMEFA

Are you not coming, then?

SARATU

I shall follow you in a while.

EMEFA

Very well, sister. I shall see you. In a while.

[*As he reaches the door she hurries over and hugs
him.*]

[*We see* PETERU *flattened against the wall, sliding
surreptitiously into the room.*]

[SARATU *and* EMEFA *break their hug.*]

EMEFA

Faith, sister. Faith.

> [PETERU *bursts in, clutching at his knife.*]

EMEFA

Brother Peteru.

PETERU

[*sheepishly*] I, um . . . came to say how much faith we all have in you, Prophet, sir. That's all.

> [*He stares strangely at the knife in his hands as if it's just been planted there. He flees, shaking his head apologetically.*]

EMEFA

I hear the murmurings of the flock, sister. I must make a move now. They are already celebrating.

> [*He leaves.*]

> [*Blackout.*]

END OF ACT THREE

EPILOGUE

SARATU

A thunderous roar went up among the crowd when he stepped out the door. The sun caught him by the neck and formed a circle around his head. His cassock danced gently in the breeze. His face gleamed—he wasn't sweating, but his face gleamed. There was silence as he walked slowly towards the gates of the vicarage. Some say it was like the day Ogun came down from his hill, clothed in fire and wearing a garment of blood; and they immediately made him king. The crowd was lined up on both sides of the road, and even on the road itself, so that it was almost impossible to find a path through the thick surge of bodies. But they made way for him. Instinctively, they moved back and made a path for him. He looked straight ahead as he walked through them. Straight ahead. He did not look to the left. Nor to the right. They tried to read his face, to fathom his thoughts. But he was impenetrable. He walked regally, slowly. And the sun, like a shadow, followed his movement.

The zoo was already open when he reached the gates. It was only then that he paused and looked back at the crowd. There was awe and worship and trembling in them when he looked back. As the zoo-keeper, who was himself shaking uncontrollably, closed the gates after him and handed him the keys to the cage, a loud sigh went up among the crowd.

Again, as he walked through the zoo, he looked neither left nor right. Only straight ahead. Again, when he got to the cage he was looking for, he paused at the gate and looked behind his shoulder. Many in the crowd were practically glued to the grilled fences of the zoo. Some had even found positions on trees around.

He inserted the key in the lock. Turned it twice, and pushed it in. He locked it behind him when he entered, raised the bunch of keys in the air for the crowd to see, and gently flung it out of the cage. Then he turned and headed for the beast.

It was having a nap when he came up to it. Sleeping lazily with its belly up to the sun. He made the sign of the cross, murmured a few words of prayer and lay his hand upon its head. It woke up and looked sleepily at him. They stared at each other for a while. In a contest of wills.

[*Pause.*]

Miraculously, he won. It went flat on its stomach as if in greeting. He turned to the crowd and allowed himself a tiny smile. "Behold another Daniel," he said. "Behold a Daniel." A wild cheer went up. The air was filled with cries of "Amen, Amen, Amen."

The photographers clicked away. People rolled on the ground, taken by the spirit. He simply stood there, one hand gently on the beast, and the half-smile at the corners of his mouth.

No-one saw the precise moment it leapt at him. No-one remembers. Not even the cameras caught it.

[*Instant blackout. A succession of slide shots leaps out at us from the darkness. The first one reads: . . . Afterwards they said the lion had thought it was being served an early dinner. The next one reads:Was it suicide? Was he under the influence of a spell? Had he simply taken leave of his senses? The next one reads: "Regarding Emefa": The Coroner's Verdict. Next week . . . Only in our Sunday Supplement . . . Book in advance with your vendor . . .]*

SARATU

Death catches the hunter with pain.
    Eshu catches the swimmer in water.
When the tapper fell to his death
    He was cleansed with wine, bathed in its froth.
He rested at the foot of a palm;
    He was remembered in songs.
He became a God.

[*Blackout.*]

THE END

ME AND THE BOYS

Characters

KAS

MO

Me and the Boys was first presented at the Finborough
Theatre, Earls Court, London, on 19 July 1995 as part of
the London New Play Festival. It was directed by David
Prescott with the following cast:

KAS . . . . . Evroy Deer

MO . . . . . Karl Collins

Lights rise on KAS, *a young man in his early thirties, and* MO, *about ten years younger. It should gradually become clear that the two men are in a prison cell.*

KAS

Sit back, relax, let me tell you a story. It wasn't one of those painfully beautiful days when the blue sky . . . [*pulls out from his pocket a pack of cigarettes*] . . . et cetera, right?

> [*He offers* MO *a cigarette.* MO *hesitates with an 'are you sure' countenance. Reassured, he accepts the cigarette. They light up.*]

I mean, the sun outside—let me tell you about that sun. It was something else, it was so hot even refrigerators were melting. I mean, that's how hot it was. I mean, it was like the sun had some personal bone to pick with us. But the breeze, Jesuschrist, the breeze. It was like an air-conditioner. You grab? You get the picture? It was that kind of day when all self-respecting students said "to hell with lectures, let's go have a beer". That's how come we were at the student union bar that afternoon, me and the boys, knocking back the beers, puffing at the good old B&Hs. There were five of us. There was me, not the me you're seeing now. I'm talking of a young, handsome me. I'm talking—if that me walked in through that door right now you wouldn't even think we were from the same planet never mind being one and the same. I'm going back years now, you know, way back. Anyway, there was me, there was Je (who is now a big-time defence attorney, specializing in politicians and corpo-

army officer; GG, who died in a car crash two days later. And Wuyi, whose claim to fame was that he could drink anyone under the table, go into an exam with the mother of all hangovers and still come out tops. What made it worse was that he just didn't give a hoot. I mean, that guy was so bright, he just didn't give a shit. I mean, some guys—me, for instance—I studied four weeks for a test once. I'm telling you, four weeks of no sleep, no booze, no girls, no nothing—and you know what? I still failed the goddam test. But Wuyi—let me tell you something about Wuyi: he couldn't read. That guy couldn't read. Don't get me wrong, he wasn't, you know . . . what's that word for people who can't read? Illiterate? Not that one. Dyspeptic? Not that one either. But you know the one I mean, it starts with a d. Anyway, it wasn't that Wuyi couldn't read, he just hated reading. And yet give him an exam paper and he'd make the questions feel stupid. I hated him for that. I mean, where's the justice? Where's the fucking justice? I swear to God, man. So, there was me, Bosco, Wuyi, GG and Je. Je—let me tell you about Je. He wasn't bunking off anything that day. He had nothing to bunk off as he'd been chucked out from the university only a few weeks after that *mea culpa* affair. He—oh, did I tell you about that *mea culpa* affair?

[MO *does not react.*]

Let me tell you about the *mea culpa* affair. It was like this: Je was studying law, right? And Latin was a must for all law students. Anyway, Je is sitting for his mid-semester Latin exam, right? I mean, he's just sat down and looked at the questions, and the first one—you know what it says?—it says: translate *mea culpa*. And you know what the goat-head wrote down? (a) Why? (b) Who cares? Just for fun, you know, just for a laugh. Next thing

cares? Just for fun, you know, just for a laugh. Next thing we know he's been invited to appear before the Senate—that's the, you know, disciplinary board—to explain himself. The hearing was to take place at 8 a.m. on a Monday morning. But what does my friend do the night before his hearing? He throws a party for his girlfriend, Teray. He had no choice really, it was her birthday. Anyway, he went to bed at 5 a.m., slept through the alarm clock and woke up—ask me when he woke up?—

[MO *is silent.*]

—after midday, that's when he woke up. That didn't stop the Senate hearing from going ahead though. They simply voted to kick him out, period. Just like that, God's case no appeal. I mean, those professors, man, they're real fuckers. I mean, to expel someone just like that, no trial, no nothing. That's why this country is in trouble today. I mean, you know? Anyway, that's how come Je was kicked out. So, now he just hung out on campus, you know, with us, basically chilling out until the next academic year when his mum, a Lagos tycoon who'd been classmates with the First Lady, was bound to persuade the Senate to reconsider their decision (which they did, the wankers, I'm glad to say). So Je was up there with us that day, at the bar on the first floor of the students union building only because he had nothing better to do while waiting for his girlfriend to join him after lectures. Now, Je and Teray, they were something else. They were so bad. I mean, to see them snuggling up the way they always did, you'd think falling in love was going out of fashion, I mean, like it was some illegal substance. I mean, it was *deep*, man. I mean—you get my point?—it was disgusting. I mean, so fucking beautiful. I mean, beautiful to the point of disgusting. I mean, I envied those two like fuck.

So there we were at the bar, chilling out on beer and
cigs—music in the background and all that shit, you
know—and basically jiving about this and that. You
know, just like me and you right now, just jiving. I don't
remember now how our conversation swerved from girls
and politics to the topic of Heaven and Hell. But it did,
and that's what this story is all about.

[*Pause.*]

"According to the Bible, or the Quran, or some such other
Holy writ, it is in the best interests of every creature on
earth to aspire to Heaven." That's how Wuyi began his
sudden outburst. No provocation, no nothing. His eyes
just went red—like traffic lights. I mean, if he'd gone and
stood in the middle of a road with those eyes, cars
would've stopped and waited for him to turn green.

[MO *smiles.*]

You think it's funny? I don't blame you, you're a small
boy. All I can say is, I pray nobody ever looks at you the
way Wuyi looked at us that day. It was a Bad-Luck look,
man. I mean, anyway, I opened my mouth to protest. But
he emptied an entire whole pint of Guinness down my
throat. Call it bribery, call it intimidation: it shut me up.
The others pointedly studied the soles of their shoes.
"Heaven, by the way," he continued, as if he was talking
to a group of complete idiots, "is where people like Jesus
the Christ, Mohammed the Prophet, Bhudda the Lord,
and a host of other strange bed-fellows have been living
in cordiality for the past two or three thousand years
while their followers here on earth have hardly ever
taken time off from slaying one another. Heaven is where
nothing ever goes wrong, death doesn't exist, happiness
overflows, love is the catchword, night never falls: it's
like one of those movies in which the good guy finally

wins the heart of the beautiful heroine while the baddie
gets run over by a donkey. The bad guy, of course, goes
to Hell. Hell, by the way, is where mama says papa will
go whenever he comes home speaking Esperanto, break-
dancing and swearing that he isn't drunk."

One other thing you could say for that Wuyi of a guy is
that the man knew how to blow grammar. I mean, him
and grammar was born on the same day. He paused to
light a cigarette then he went on. "Every Sunday morning, this group of preachers come knocking. It's this
Heaven and Hell palaver." GG snatched the cigarette
from him, cussed him for always sponging off other
people's cigarettes and then stormed out of the bar.

[*Pause.*]

That was the last time we saw GG alive. Of course we
had no way of knowing this at the time, or I'm sure Wuyi
wouldn't have told him to "fuck off, you holier-than-us,
bless-me-father-for-I-have-sinned, oh-I'm-so-holy-and-
so-Christian-prick". But we didn't, and Wuyi said it. He
lit another cigarette. From my pack this time. The bar
was filling up as per usual, guys were checking in, and
some girls too. Je's eyes were fixed on the door, on the
look-out for his woman Teray. For one tiny moment of
sheer bloody-mindedness I hoped she didn't turn up. But
Je was my pal, and not such a bad one at that, so I began
to look out too, my heart doing a tango every time a girl
entered the bar.

[MO *smiles.*]

The first time the preachers came around, said Wuyi,
they asked him: "Five minutes after you're dead, where
do you think you'd be?" "Hopefully in a morgue," he
replied. They decided to rephrase their question. "When
you die, where do you think you'd go—Heaven or Hell?"

At first he wanted to ask them what on earth they thought the earth was: what with the millions dying of starvation, wars everywhere, people getting fucked by governments all over and . . . (that was when Bosco chipped in with some silly-arse remark about it must be hell too for Je having to wait so long for his girlfriend. I mean—you know what I mean—he was only kidding, right?) But the way Wuyi reacted! I mean, he went fucking crazy! I mean, I just thought, what the fuck! I mean, have you ever been stopped in the middle of the night in the middle of nowhere by a drunken policeman with an AK47? And you think, shit, this zombie is going to shoot me. That's how he looked that evening, Wuyi. I tell you—like a fucking AK. That's when I began to get worried. He swung on Bosco and said, in this tone that was so calm you knew it was the, ah, the mouth . . . the tip of a, ah, volcano. "What do you know about having girlfriends, Bosco?" I thought, oho. Because I knew what he was driving at, right? And Bosco's the kind of guy who never takes shit from anybody, right? I just thought, oho. I mean, when AK47 jam Uzi, what do you get? Bloodbath at Lobster Bay . . . [*demonstrates a shoot-out*] . . . that's what. So I thought, oho. But, what does Bosco say? He says nothing. Just sits there smiling, right? This smile that says nothing, right? And you know what they say about the man who says nothing: fear the motherfucker. And Wuyi goes again: "I mean it, what do you know about having girlfriends?" Still Bosco doesn't say a word. The only sign that he's listening is that his nose begins to twitch. [*demonstrates*] Like this. "Leave him alone," I said to Wuyi. He didn't even seem to hear me. "The last girlfriend you went out with had a beard and a dick, that's what I mean," he said to Bosco. There was a long silence around the table as Bosco slowly finished his beer. Then he stood up. Just like that, not a word, nothing, and went out the door. That's when I started breathing again.

"You've got a mouth the size of a pit latrine," Je said to Wuyi. He shrugged. "He shouldn't have come up with that silly-arse remark." But Je was really pissed off. "I'm out of here the moment Teray comes through that door," he said. "What makes you think she will?" Wuyi asked, and began to laugh. Je's eyes lit up. "Don't mess with me, Wuyi." "The problem with little shits like you," responded Wuyi, "is that you wear stupidity and mistake it for a crash helmet." I told them to stop it. "He started it first," said Je. "No, you started it," said Wuyi. "All because I was trying, like a good friend, to tell you that your dear sweetheart is cutting shows with one of her lecturers." Through the corner of my eye I saw Je snatch a bottle off the table. I knocked it out of his hand and grabbed both his wrists. Wuyi was rolling on the floor, laughing till his eyes watered. "You scared me, man. I'm trembling with fright. By the way, the lecturer's name is Labisi. He's in Sociology."

Je was asthmatic. He started breathing heavily like he was choking or something. I dipped into his pocket and brought out his inhaler. He spritzed a couple of times. I gave Wuyi an evil look. "Okay, I'm sorry," he said, without the faintest hint of being sorry. I asked Je if he wanted to go back to the digs and wait there for Teray. He shook his head, said he was fine. He caught the barman's eye. "Anyone for more beer?" Wuyi accepted the offer without batting an eyelid and continued his story about the preachers. "Excuse me, I said to them." He said he said to them, "I'm sorry, but I don't think I want to go to Heaven. None of my friends will be there."

And then he became quiet. We waited for him to go on.
But that was it, that was the end of his story. Then he
stood up and began to dance. There was no music—the
sound system had gone quiet—but man, he didn't give a
damn, he didn't need the sound system. He just got up
from that table, put his arms around someone only he
could see, someone invisible, pulled them very close, and
began this weird, slow, beautiful dance. I mean, it was
so beautiful.

[*Pause.*]

Then he got down on his knees—you know, like a puppy
—and started sniffing the dust on the floor like, you
know, a puppy.

[*Pause.*]

He's still in a nuthouse even as we speak right now, ten
years later. That's how long I've been in this place myself.
Ten years, man, ten fucking years. They claimed I'd been
his dealer, you see, that I'd sold him some way-out stuff
that fucked up his mind. I just don't know, man. The way
I see it, a man's got to make a living, but that stuff that
fucked Wuyi up didn't come from me. I swear by my
mother's grave. I mean, I was only trying to make some
little bread on the side, right? I mean, I didn't walk up
to anybody and put a knife to their neck or anything,
right? But you know why I got picked? Why they picked
me? Because I was a nobody. My folks were Mr and Mrs
Nobody. They had to pick on someone, so they picked me.
Fucked up my life, man. Flushed my whole entire future
down a toilet.

Enough about me. What are you inside for?

[MO *makes to speak but is immediately cut short
by* KAS.]

You know what I wanted to be? What I really wanted to be? A coup-plotter, that's what. Get my degree, join the army, that was my dream. That was the plan. Join the goddam army and lead a coup, shake up the whole goddam system. I'll tell you this for nothing, my friend: you're looking at the best president this country never had. My man GG—you know, the one who died in a car crash—he had a saying, he used to say: life's a weird story, and then it stops. I say, life's a bitch. Now, let me tell you a secret: the stuff GG was on the night he drove his car under a truck? He bought it from me. I still feel bad about the way he died like that. I mean, really bad. I mean, I'm talking nightmares here, man. I mean, he was like a sister to me, man. Sometimes though I wonder what really pains me most: the fact that he died, or the fact that he died without paying for that stuff I sold him on credit. I mean, it wasn't mine to give away. I mean, you know.

[*Pause.*]

Pass me the matches, will you?

[*Slow fade to black.*]

THE END

Other plays by 'Biyi Bandele
MARCHING FOR FAUSA

"Nigerian 'Biyi Bandele's first full-length play simply crackles with anger and dark laughter. It is a story of terror and corruption in an African state: a journalist investigates a shady cabinet minister with predictable results. It's as if Dario Fo had written a fiery and ferocious political parable. Highly recommended."

John Peter, The Sunday Times

RESURRECTIONS

"Bandele is an extraordinarily talented writer who needs no special pleading. *Resurrections* is a work which resonates with ideas about history and heroism, set in a modern-day African state where ancient legends still abide. Drug-dealers, lawyers, ghosts and vultures mingle on stage, and all seem equally convincing . . . 'This is Kafka on speed,' says one of the confused spirits. Actually, it's much better than Kafka. *Resurrections* is a visual and verbal treat from a gifted writer still at the beginning of what will doubtless be a long and fruitful career."

Louise Doughty, The Mail on Sunday

TWO HORSEMEN

"In *Two Horsemen* 'Biyi Bandele writes sympathetically about imaginative escape from drudgery. Two men in a hut while away the time talking. They say they are street-sweepers, but gradually they slither away from reality, swapping identities and repeating passages of dialogue until you have no idea who they are, what is the truth and whether they are alive or dead. Bandele's writing is exciting, enigmatic and disturbing — like Beckett and Pinter, he manages to use dramatic dialogue to create an unsettling slippery world."

Sarah Hemming, The Independent

For a free copy of our complete list of plays and theatre books write to: AMBER LANE PRESS, Church Street, Charlbury, Oxford OX7 3PR Telephone and fax: 01608 810024